MR. MAC-A-DOODLE, YOU'RE A GENIUS

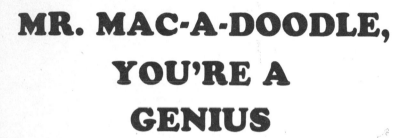

a book of numbers

Written by Marian Frances   Illustrated by Veronica Buffington

Troll Associates

Mr. Mac-a-Doodle

had a

farm.

My farm is wonderful,
thought Mr. Mac-a-Doodle.

I have a house.

And I have my animals...

all where they belong.

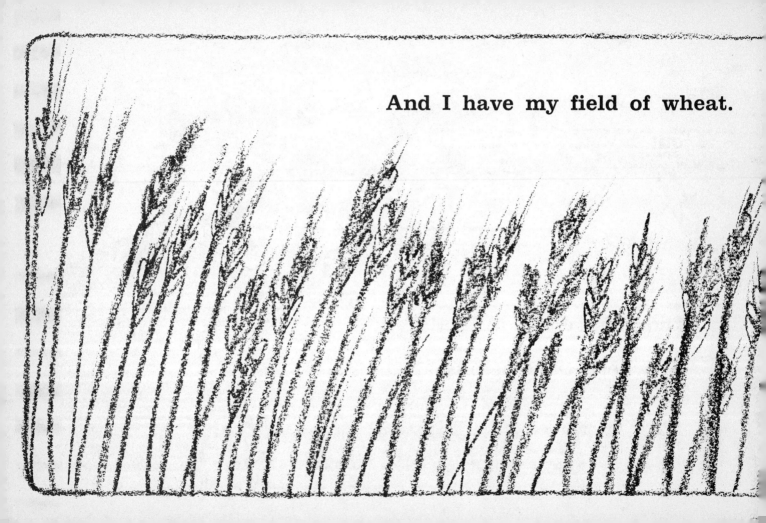

And I have my field of wheat.

I even have a big red tractor
to cut my wheat.

But Mr. Mac-a-Doodle was not content.

In fact

he was

quite sad.

My barn is just too small!

Then Mr. Mac-a-Doodle had a wonderful idea.

I will stretch my barn to make it big!

Mr. Mac-a-Doodle put Henrietta
in the barn.

one mooing cow

But nothing happened.

So Mr. Mac-a-Doodle put two horses in the barn.

2 two wide-eyed horses

Nothing happened. Then Mr. Mac-a-Doodle put

three woolly lambs in the barn.

BAAA
BAAA

BAAA

3

three

baaa,

baaa,

baaaing

lambs

Nothing happened.

Then Mr. Mac-a-Doodle

put four

huffy, gruffy

goats

in the barn.

4   four gruffy goats

Nothing happened.

Finally Mr. Mac-a-Doodle

put five fat cats

in the barn.

5   five frolicky, colicky cats

Then Mr. Mac-a-Doodle heard a strange and wonderful sound:

C-R-E-A-K
CREAK
CREAK

My barn is finally

beginning to grow,

thought Mr. Mac-a-Doodle.

C-r-e-a-k.   C-r-e-a-k.

But Mr. Mac-a-Doodle was still
not satisfied. So he put six beagles
in the barn.

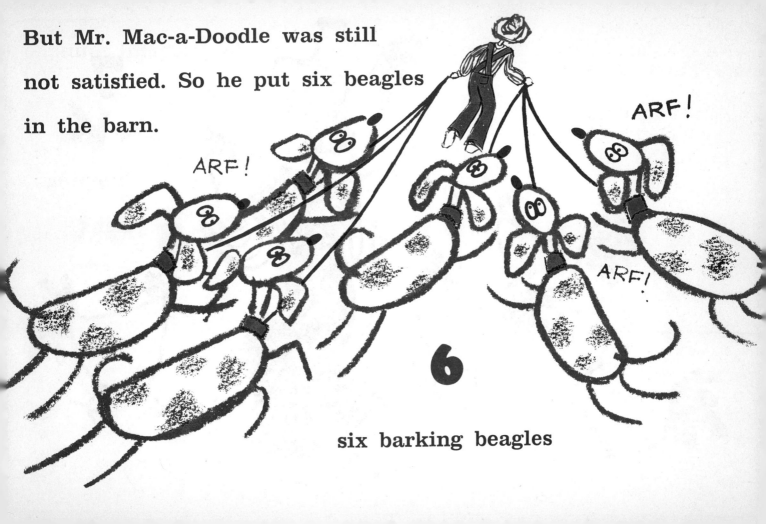

six barking beagles

Then he put
seven hens
in the barn.

7

seven

hopping

hens

C-r-e-a-k. C-r-e-a-k. Mr. Mac-a-Doodle was really
on the right track.   He put eight crowing roosters
in the barn.

8

COCK-A-DOODLE-DO !

eight roosters

Then Mr. Mac-a-Doodle put nine plump pigs in the barn.

9

nine oinking pigs

And finally,

to make his barn really grow,

Mr. Mac-a-Doodle put in ten bumblebees.

BUZZZZZZZZZZZZZZ

10   ten buzzing bees

"Mrs. Mac-a-Doodle.

Mrs. Mac-a-Doodle,"

called Mr. Mac-a-Doodle.

"Come quick.

I have stretched my barn to make it grow.'

C-R-E-A-K

CREAK

Mrs. Mac-a-Doodle

hurried to the barn

and this is

what she saw —

"Oh, Mr. Mac-a-Doodle. A mistake.
A mistake," said Mrs. Mac-a-Doodle.

"You have not made your barn
grow bigger... just too tight!"

Well, Mr. Mac-a-Doodle was the kind of man who knew how to fix a mistake.

He opened the barn door.

Out buzzed ten bumblebees **10**

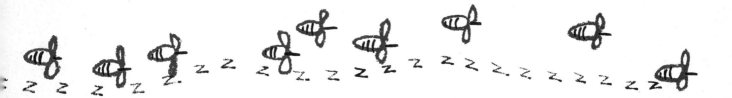

and nine oinking pigs. **9**

seven hopping hens,

7

six barking beagles

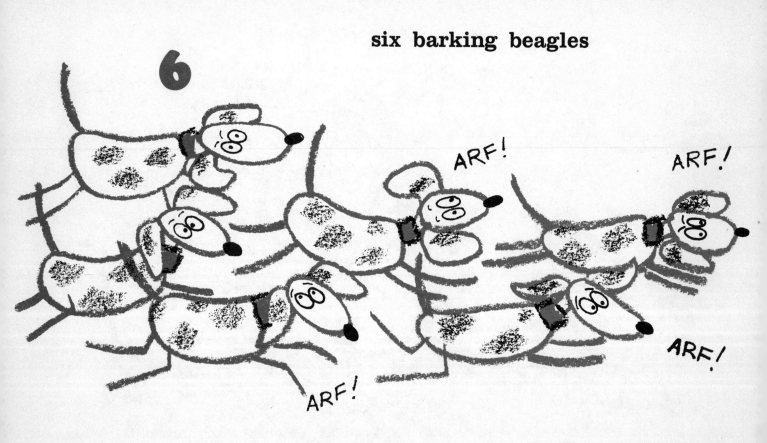

and five colicky cats.

5

Four gruffy goats

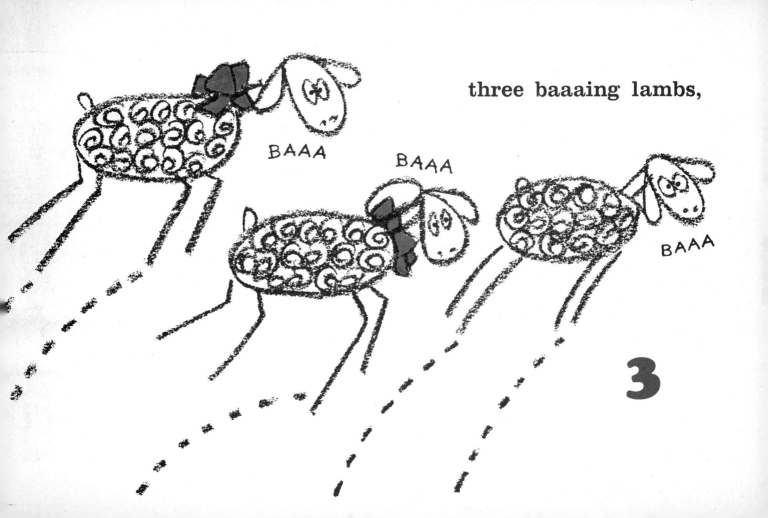

three baaaing lambs,

and two wide-eyed horses.

2

Then Mr. Mac-a-Doodle closed the barn door.

He had a new idea!

Hello, Henrietta. You stay in!

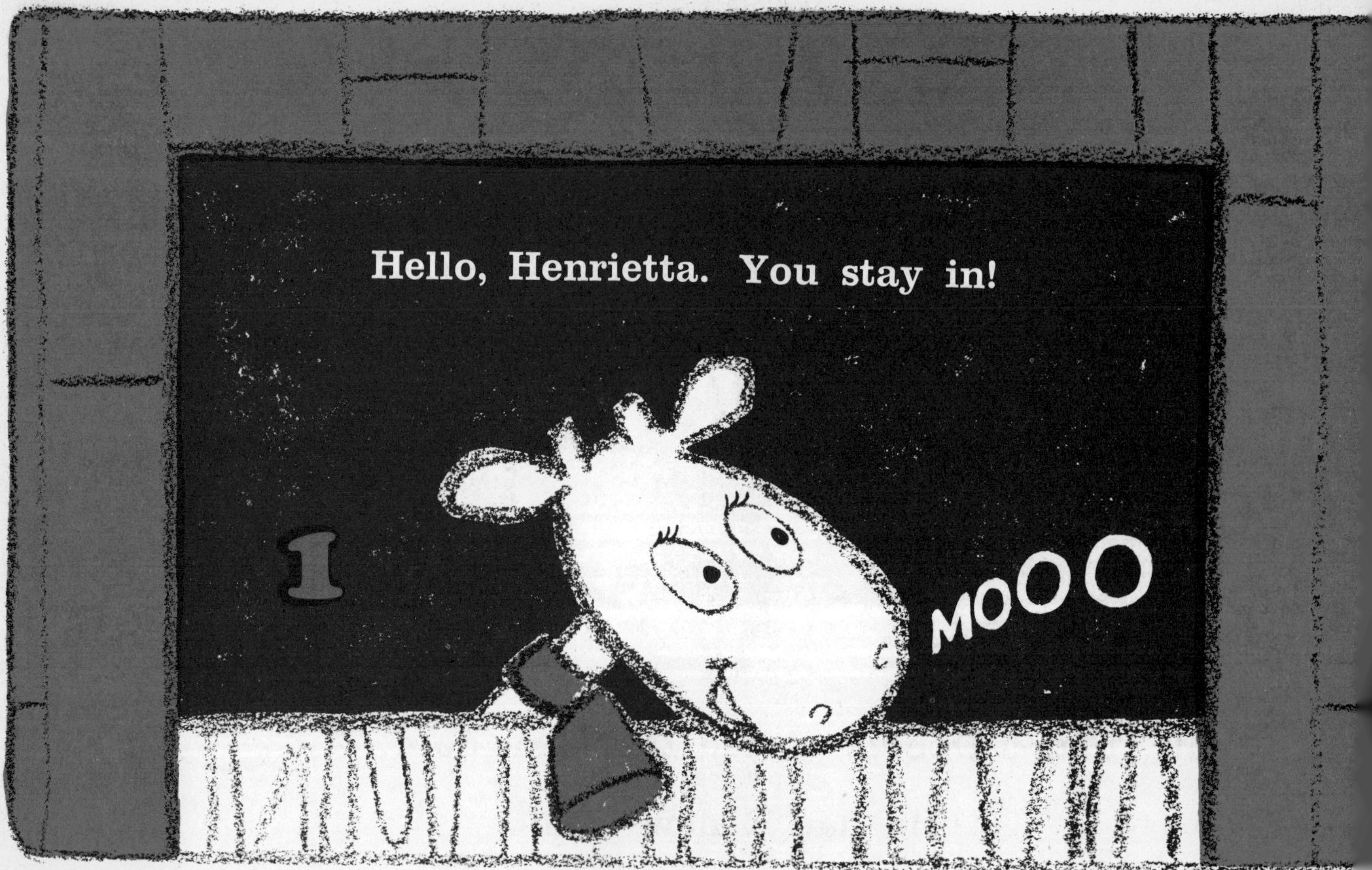

Now I have a
perfect barn...
not too big
and not too tight —
just right.
A perfect home
for Henrietta.

"Oh, Mr. Mac-a-Doodle.

You are a genius,"

said Mrs. Mac-a-Doodle.

MOOOO